# Once Upon a Baby Brother

Sarah Sullivan

Pictures by
Tricia Tusa

Farrar Straus Giroux ❧ New York

To storytellers everywhere, especially my friends at Vermont College,
and to Melanie Kroupa, with gratitude
—S.S.

For Melanie, topped with glitter and
merry treeballs
—T.T.

Text copyright © 2010 by Sarah Sullivan
Pictures copyright © 2010 by Tricia Tusa
All rights reserved
Distributed in Canada by D&M Publishers, Inc.
Color separations by Embassy Graphics Ltd.
Printed in October 2009 in China by Leo Paper, Heshan City, Guangdong Province
Designed by Jaclyn Sinquett
First edition, 2010
10  9  8  7  6  5  4  3  2  1

www.fsgkidsbooks.com

Library of Congress Cataloging-in-Publication Data
Sullivan, Sarah.
    Once upon a baby brother / Sarah Sullivan ; pictures by Tricia Tusa.— 1st ed.
      p.  cm.
    Summary: Lizzie, who loves to tell and write stories, is surprised to discover that much
of her storytelling inspiration comes from her messy baby brother.
    ISBN: 978-0-374-34635-5
    [1. Storytelling—Fiction.   2. Creative writing—Fiction.   3. Brothers and sisters—
Fiction.   4. Babies—Fiction.]   I. Tusa, Tricia, ill.   II. Title.

PZ7.S95355On 2010
[E]—dc22
                                                                    2008016791

From the day she could talk, Lizzie loved to tell stories. Tall ones. True ones. Funny ones. Sad ones. Lizzie loved them all.

She entertained the people in her mother's office.
*And the little girl grew up to be President and brought
her parents to live with her in the White House.*

She made up fairy tales to share with her father during their hikes up Mount Tilapia.

*After slaying dragons in the forest, the princess gave a surprise birthday party for the king.*

She spun yarns for Big George.

*The beautiful girl and her handsome dog took a rocket to the moon and discovered a new planet in the solar system.*

Everything was fine UNTIL

her little brother, Marvin, came along.

When Lizzie tried to tell a story before breakfast, her mother said "Not now, dear. Marvin has a dirty diaper."

When she tried to tell her father a story after dinner, he said, "Maybe later, Lizzie. It's time for Marvin's bath."

Luckily for Lizzie, Big George still loved her stories. He would listen for hours. Stories about dogs were his favorite.

The faithful Labrador rescued his master from the storm-tossed seas.
"Arf! Arf!"

When Lizzie started second grade, she discovered that her teacher, Miss Pennyroyal, loved stories, too. All the kids in Miss Pennyroyal's class got to write stories and take turns reading them out loud.

*The brave young girl rescued her teacher from the alligator pit.*

Lizzie loved Miss Pennyroyal's second grade.

At home, Marvin loved his big sister, Lizzie.

He helped her make her bed.

He helped her brush her teeth.

He even shared his oatmeal.

Lizzie couldn't wait to get to school every morning.

At school, Miss Pennyroyal taught her students how to create interesting characters. "Think about what makes your character different from everybody else," she said, "and describe that in your stories."

Easy peasy, thought Lizzie.

She got out her Princess Merriweather pencil. While the other kids brainstormed, Lizzie started writing.

She wrote all through recess.

She was still writing while the other kids ate lunch.

"Can I go first, please?" Lizzie asked when it was time to share stories out loud.

*"There's only one creature with footprints like this, Captain."*
*"You don't mean . . ."*
*"I'm afraid so, sir. The Yeti is on the rampage again."*

"Nice to see you using those new vocabulary words," said Miss Pennyroyal.

"Thank you," said Lizzie.

The next day, while Lizzie was at school, Marvin found a tube of golden glitter glue in Lizzie's desk drawer. He made golden glitter swirls all over her favorite stuffed bear, Sebastian. Lizzie was not amused.

"Big sisters need to be patient," said Lizzie's mother.

"Babies can't help making messes," said Lizzie's father.

Lizzie curled up in her bedroom with her Imagination Notebook and wrote a new story.

Once there was a beautiful princess who lived in a castle by the Sea. She made her parents very happy. THEN the ugly prince was born.

He cried ALL the time. And made lots of messes.

So the beautiful princess banished the ugly prince to a desert island. "This castle is getting way too crowded," she told her trusty steed.

Lizzie was happy to go to school the next day.

The kids in Miss Pennyroyal's class were still writing stories about interesting characters.

Lizzie had tons of ideas. It was hard to find time to write them all down.

Run for your lives!
It's the Marvinosaurus.

Marvin's the nastiest pirate that ever sailed the sea.

Watch your fingers!
There's a Marvinfish circling below.

"I don't believe I've ever heard of a Marvinfish," said Miss Pennyroyal. "It must be very rare."

"Oh, it is," said Lizzie. "You hardly ever see one."

On Friday, Lizzie's mother announced she was taking Marvin to visit Gramma. "I hope you won't miss your little brother too much," she said.

**NO MARVIN!!**

Lizzie was thrilled.

After spaghetti for dinner, she and her father played a long game of checkers.
The next afternoon, Lizzie sharpened a whole box of pencils.
She dusted the furniture in her Princess Merriweather Magic Castle.
She rearranged the stuffed animals on her bed twelve times.
But something was missing.

At school, Miss Pennyroyal announced a new project.

"Now that we know about creating characters, we're going to write our own comic books," she said. "Everyone needs to think of a character who will have lots of adventures."

Lizzie took out her Princess Merriweather pencil.

She doodled.

She stared out the window.

For the first time, she couldn't think of a single idea.

That night, while Lizzie's father worked on a sales report for his meeting, Lizzie tried to work on her comic book.

She drew stars on the cover of her Imagination Notebook.

She stared at a liver-shaped spot on the ceiling.

She even cleaned out her sock drawer.

"Once, in a far-off galaxy," she wrote.

And then . . .

nothing!

The next day at school, the kids in Miss Pennyroyal's class turned in their comic book projects—everyone except Lizzie.

"Remember, the deadline is the day after tomorrow," said Miss Pennyroyal.

"I know," Lizzie moaned.

"Maybe you need fresh inspiration," said Miss Pennyroyal.

"Maybe," said Lizzie.

She chewed on the end of her Princess Merriweather pencil.

"It was a dark and stormy night," she wrote, and then . . .

nothing!

At home, Lizzie looked for inspiration.

She listened to music and drew pictures on blank sheets of paper.

She reread her favorite fairy tales.

She studied the comics in the Sunday paper.

Nothing helped.

"I'll never think of a character for my comic book," Lizzie moaned.

She went downstairs for a glass of juice.
"Mug worts," said the chrysanthemum.
"Marvin?" said Lizzie. "When did you get home?"

"Ziff wizzle," said Marvin. Then
he knocked over Lizzie's juice.
"Oh, Marvin!" said Lizzie.
"Loops," said Marvin.

Lizzie thought about Miss
Pennyroyal's instructions:
interesting characters . . .
lots of adventures . . . Hmmm.

Lizzie carried her Princess Merriweather pencil upstairs.

She wrote until bedtime and while she was brushing her teeth.

She was still writing during recess the next day.
"Is your comic book ready to turn in?" asked Miss Pennyroyal.
"Not quite," said Lizzie. "I need to show it to someone at home first."
"As long as you turn it in tomorrow," said Miss Pennyroyal.

While her mother cooked dinner, Lizzie pulled
Marvin into her lap.

"Listen to this," she said.

"ALIENS have landed. They're taking over the city."

Out of the sky swooped the Amazing Marvin with Big George the Wonder Dog.

Marvin sprayed the tiny villains with paralyzing purple slime.

Lizzie gave Marvin a hug.
Big George lifted his chin and howled.
"That's only the beginning," said Lizzie.

"Wait till you see what happens in Episode Two!